Replacement costs will be
billed after 42 days overdue.

Is There Really a Human *RACE?*

By Jamie Lee Curtis

Illustrated by Laura Cornell

JOANNA COTLER BOOKS
An Imprint of HarperCollinsPublishers

Thanks to Tom for being the starter, my Teammates—
Joanna, Laura, Phyllis, and the whole HC team—and to
Dr. Susan Williams, for keeping me on track.
—J.L.C.

Thanks to the gals, Jamie, Joanna, Karen, Alyson, Kathryn,
Lucille, and Dorothy, and to the guys, Neil and Jaime.
—L.C.

Is There Really a Human Race?

Text copyright © 2006 by Jamie Lee Curtis   Illustrations copyright © 2006 by Laura Cornell

Printed in the United State of America.   All rights reserved.

Library of Congress Cataloging-in-Publication Data

Curtis, Jamie Lee.

   Is there really a human race? / by Jamie Lee Curtis ; illustrated by Laura Cornell. — 1st ed.

      p.   cm.

   Summary: While thinking about life as a race, a child wonders whether it is most important to finish first or to have fun
along the way.

   ISBN-10: 0-06-075346-3 (trade bdg.) — ISBN-13: 978-0-06-075346-7 (trade bdg.)

   ISBN-10: 0-06-075348-X (lib. bdg.) — ISBN-13: 978-0-06-075348-1 (lib. bdg.)

   [1. Conduct of life—Fiction. 2. Stories in rhyme.] I. Cornell, Laura, ill. II. Title.

PZ8.3.C9347Ist 2006   2006000274

[E]—dc22   CIP

                                                                                                                          AC

Designed by Neil Swaab   1 2 3 4 5 6 7 8 9 10 ❖ First Edition

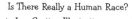

For Chris
—J.L.C.

For Lilly
—L.C.

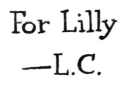

Is there really a human race?

Is it going on now all over the place?
When did it start?
Who said, "Ready, Set, Go"?

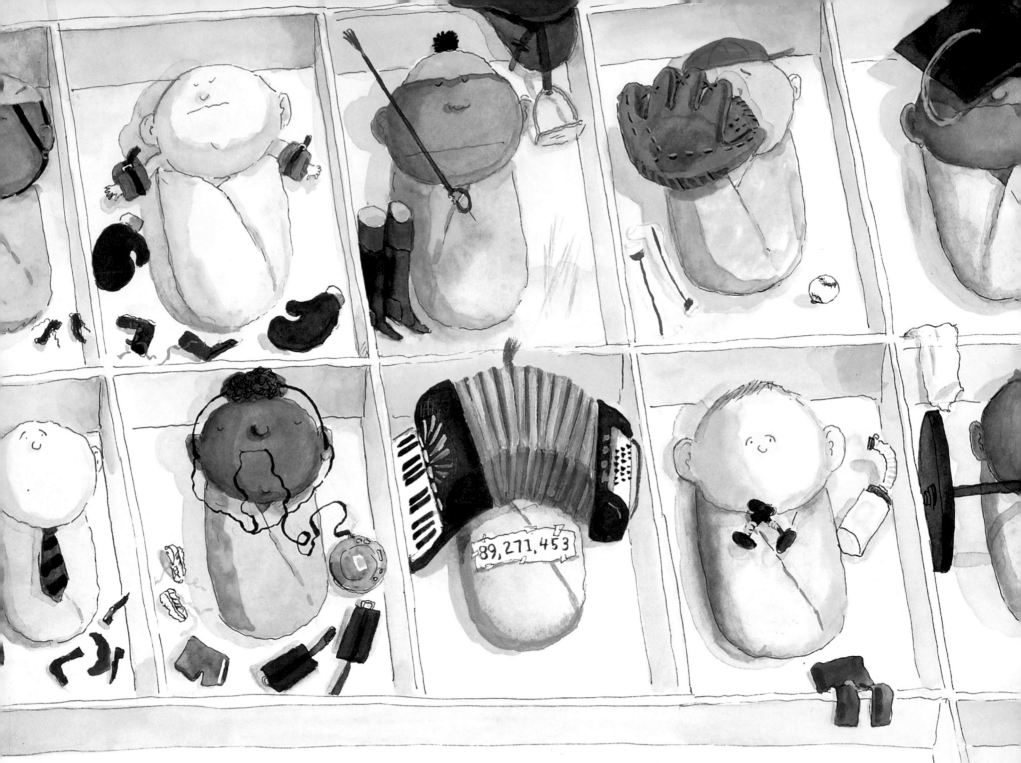

Did it start on my birthday?
I really must know.

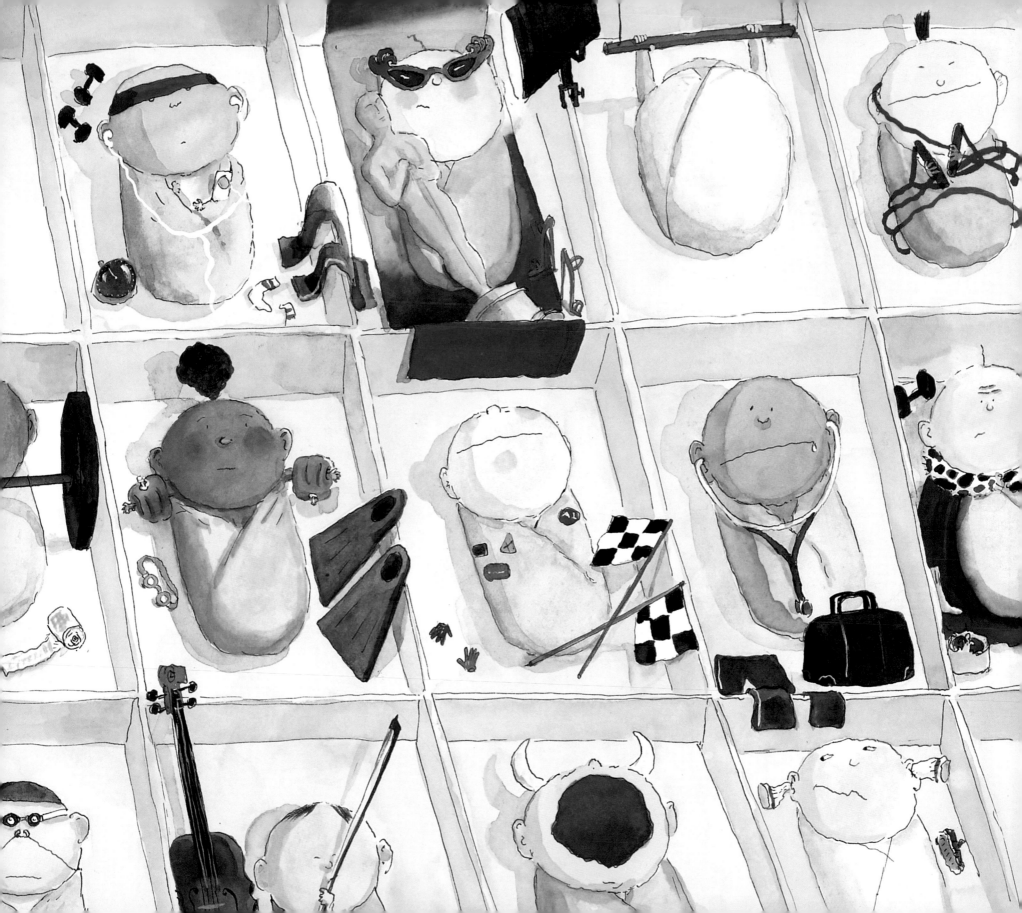

Do I practice and train?

Do I get my own coach?

Do I get my own lane?

If the race is a relay, is Dad on my team?

And **his** dad and **his** dad? You know what I mean.

Is the race like a loop
or an obstacle course?
Am I a jockey,
or am I a horse?

Is there pushing and shoving
to get to the lead?
If the race is unfair,
will I succeed?

Do some of us win? Do some of us lose?
Is winning or losing something I choose?
Why am I racing? What am I winning?
Does all of my running keep the world spinning?

If I get off track
when I take the wrong turn,
do I make my way back
from mistakes?

Do I learn?

Is it a sprint? A dash to the end?
Am I aware of the time that I spend?
And why do I do it, this zillion-yard dash?
If we don't help each other, we're all going to . . .

Sometimes it's better not to go fast.
There are beautiful sights to be seen when you're last.

Shouldn't it be that you just try your best?
And that's more important than beating the rest?

Shouldn't it be looking back at the end
that you judge your own race by the help that you lend?

So, take what's inside you and make big, bold choices.
And for those who can't speak for themselves,

use **bold** voices.

And make friends and love well,
bring art to this place.
And make the world better

for the whole

Do you have any 2's?

Go fish.

human race.

CYN-D
Aerobics instructor

RATANA
Union leader

MONA
Cosmetic Surgeon

RADKO
Furrier

BOB
Self-help author

FLAVIA
Tanning Salon

GORDON
Picnic planner

TOM
Accordionist

IVANA
Astronaut

MINH
Mud brick master

SHARICE
Professor of Irish literature

JORGE
Venture capitalist

ROSE
International affairs

WALEED
Circus clown

CHANDRAK
Tech Support

GAMBA
Allergist

LISA
Career criminal

BEA
Prison guard

ROLAND
Audrey Hepburn Fan Club

LING
Medical Aesthetics

MAURICE
Choir master

SAUL
Hotel reservations

SYLVIE
Hat designer

ROSCOE
Manicur

WORLD YEARBOOK